Dracula's Cat

Dracula's Cat

by Jan Wahl
illustrated by Kay Chorao

SIMON AND SCHUSTER BOOKS FOR YOUNG READERS
Published by Simon & Schuster Inc., New York

This is the castle where my master
Count Dracula lives. When the
moon is full it's not *wise* to go there.

"Miaoow," I tell him. "Hey! It is time to
wake up." Something howls in the woods.
Dracula rises. Out of his coffin. He should
get me my saucer of milk.

Tonight the moon is orange and big.
He forgets my milk! With his cloak
on he crawls like a lizard down the wall.
His carriage waits. Well! I had better follow...

"MER-rowww!" I cry. "*I* want to come!"
I jump fast. The carriage is pulled
by coal-black horses into the night.
Owls hoot. Dry leaves whistle in the
wind. I snuggle close to him.

The carriage stops near Mistress
Agatha's cottage. He is going to
SCARE her. I see the look in his
eyes. My master steps out. Walking
as quiet as cobwebs!

Shh! He knocks at the door. I rub
my face with my paw. Moonbeams
twinkle. Dracula changes. *Into a
wolf.* He growls. What a delicious
spooky sound it is!

A tiny window opens. Mistress
Agatha's head pokes out. Now
she cries: "Just wait a minute,
Old Dracula!" I try to warn him.
"Miaoooww!" Oh. Too late!

Mistress Agatha dumps a bucket of
pig slop on him. He shudders and
shakes. My master bays at the
moon: "Woo-OO!" Once more
changing shape. This time into—

the shape of a *bat*! Fluttering up.
Up in air! Beating his wings on
the window. I hear loud clatter of
wood shoes running THUNK! THUNK!
downstairs. Red-faced Mistress Agatha
dashes forth with a broom.

She yells, giving him a whack. "Take that, Old Dracula!" He flies off into the apple tree boughs. I follow.

My master, the bat, gets stuck in
high tree limbs. What can I do to
help? I crawl up the apple tree.

I pull. I tug. And at last I tug bat
Dracula loose! Down he glides to
the ground! Landing on toadstools.
Again he rises—*black* and *scary*.
Hurrah!

In the rattling carriage, he holds me
in his lap. He tickles my whiskers.
He strokes my fur. I *love* it. I am
carried back home. A candle is lit
in the kitchen.

He pours me a whole, huge pitcher of sweet milk. PURRR! IT'S SO COZY TO BE DRACULA'S OWN CAT!

To Jim

SIMON AND SCHUSTER BOOKS FOR YOUNG READERS
Simon & Schuster Building, Rockefeller Center
1230 Avenue of the Americas, New York, New York 10020

SIMON AND SCHUSTER BOOKS FOR YOUNG READERS
is a trademark of Simon & Schuster Inc.

Designed by Vicki Kalajian
Manufactured in the United States of America

10 9 8 7 6 5 4 3 2 1

Library of Congress Cataloging-in-Publication Data
Wahl, Jan. Dracula's cat and Frankenstein's dog. Originally
published: Dracula's cat. Englewood Cliffs, N.J. : Prentice-
Hall, © 1978. Originally published: Frankenstein's dog.
Englewood Cliffs, N.J. : Prentice-Hall, © 1977. Summary:
Dracula's cat and Frankenstein's dog give pets' eye views
of life with their masters. [1. Pets—Fiction. 2. Cats—
Fiction. 3. Dogs—Fiction. 4. Monsters—Fiction.]
I. Chorao, Kay, ill. II. Wahl, Jan. Frankenstein's dog.
1990 III. Title. PZ7.W1266Ds 1990 89-49697
ISBN 0-671-70820-1

Jan Wahl

began his career by playing
the piano for a children's radio
show in Toledo, Ohio. Next came
the creation of traveling magic
and puppet shows. His first book,
Pleasant Fieldmouse, was illustrated by
Maurice Sendak. Later successes include
the Doctor Rabbit books and the
award-winning *Humphrey's Bear*,
illustrated by William Joyce,
and dozens of other picture books
loved by parents and children all
over the world. Jan Wahl has lived
in Copenhagen and Brooklyn Heights
and now makes his home mostly in
San Miguel de Allende, Mexico.

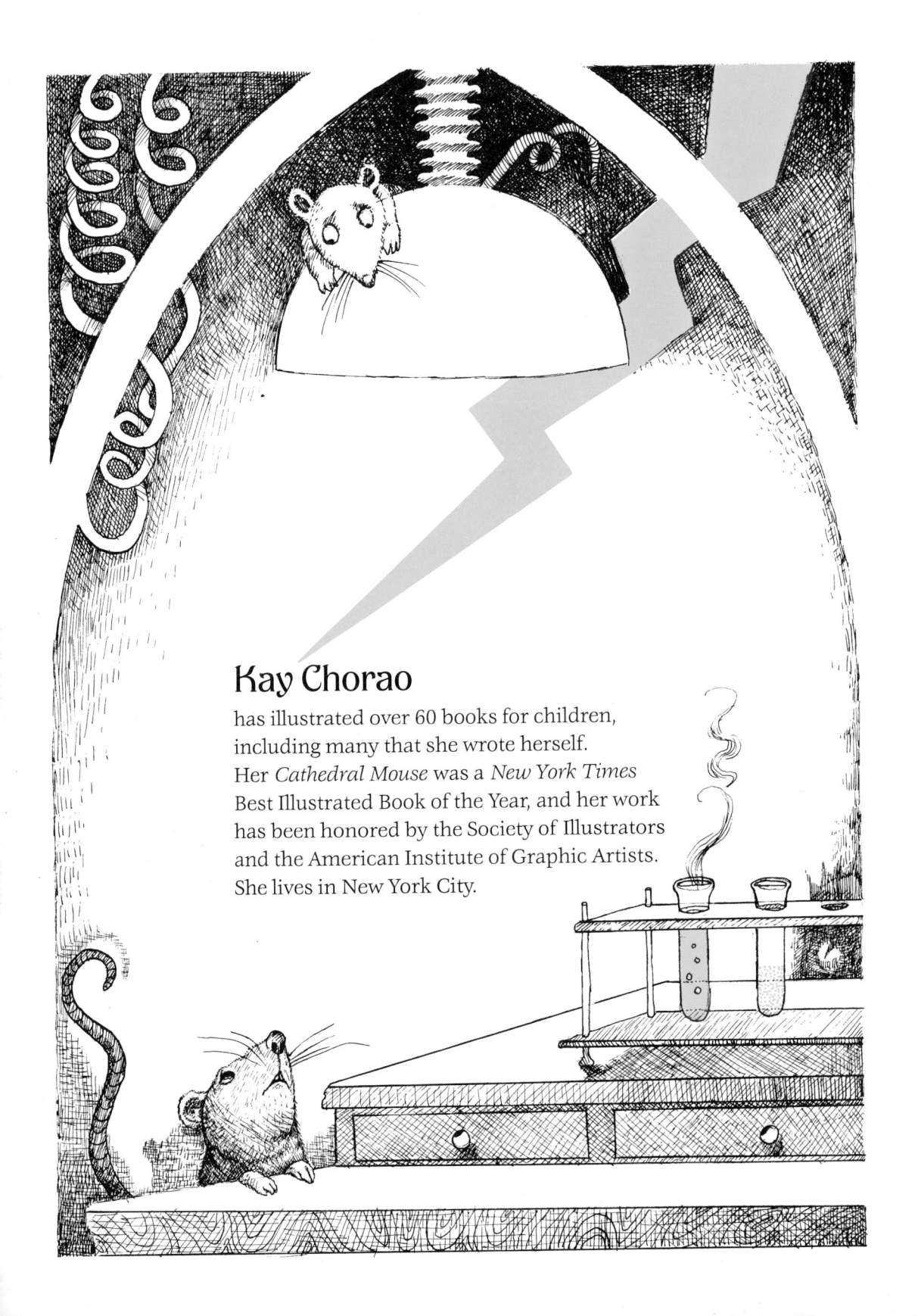

Kay Chorao

has illustrated over 60 books for children,
including many that she wrote herself.
Her *Cathedral Mouse* was a *New York Times*
Best Illustrated Book of the Year, and her work
has been honored by the Society of Illustrators
and the American Institute of Graphic Artists.
She lives in New York City.

To Andy

SIMON AND SCHUSTER BOOKS FOR YOUNG READERS
Simon & Schuster Building, Rockefeller Center
1230 Avenue of the Americas, New York, New York 10020

SIMON AND SCHUSTER BOOKS FOR YOUNG READERS
is a trademark of Simon & Schuster Inc.

Designed by Vicki Kalajian
Manufactured in the United States of America

10 9 8 7 6 5 4 3 2 1

Library of Congress Cataloging-in-Publication Data
Wahl, Jan. Dracula's cat and Frankenstein's dog. Originally
published: Dracula's cat. Englewood Cliffs, N.J. : Prentice-
Hall, © 1978. Originally published: Frankenstein's dog.
Englewood Cliffs, N.J. : Prentice-Hall, © 1977. Summary:
Dracula's cat and Frankenstein's dog give pets' eye views
of life with their masters. [1. Pets—Fiction. 2. Cats—
Fiction. 3. Dogs—Fiction. 4. Monsters—Fiction.]
I. Chorao, Kay, ill. II. Wahl, Jan. Frankenstein's dog.
1990 III. Title. PZ7.W1266Ds 1990 89-49697
ISBN 0-671-70820-1

It is time to sleep. Together we stretch
out on the hard floor. Monster and me.
Dear Monster, Good Night! SLEEP TIGHT,
DON'T LET THE BED BUGS BITE!

"Monster," I try to suggest. "Let us be *good* friends." He grunts in a strange way. We tussle. He understands.

Now it is supper-time. We each have
a bowl on the floor. Yuck. Mush again—
with paprika. *He* seems to love it!

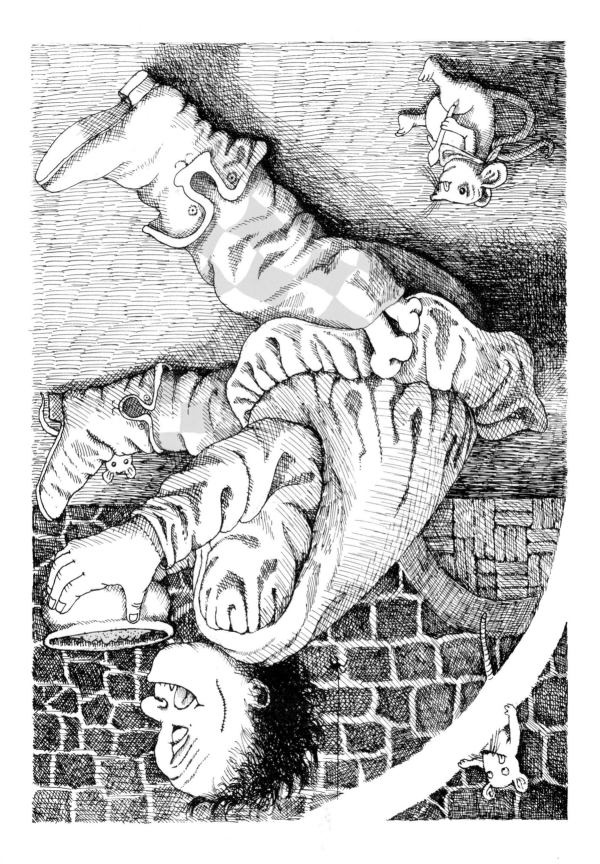

At last Frankenstein and Schnickelfritz
let us alone. I show Monster where I hide
bones. He helps me dig. I show him my
favorites. He is bigger. He takes the most.
He is smart for a monster.

Guess what? This time Monster
wants to fetch the stick. This game is
growing better! He is learning to walk.
So we try to see who gets it first.
Monster or me.

Doctor Frankenstein throws me a stick. Stupid game! I am to bring it back. All right. I bring it back. Now he throws it again! How dumb does he think I am?

The yellow sun is too shiny for his new eyes. He blinks. I guide him by taking his pants in my teeth. Slowly.

"*One, Two! One, Two!*" Do your stuff,
Mister Monster. Outside the birds are
singing. Monster waves at them and
wants to listen. He is trying to sing, also.

Doctor Frankenstein and his helper, Schnickelfritz, put poor Monster back on his feet again. Good luck!

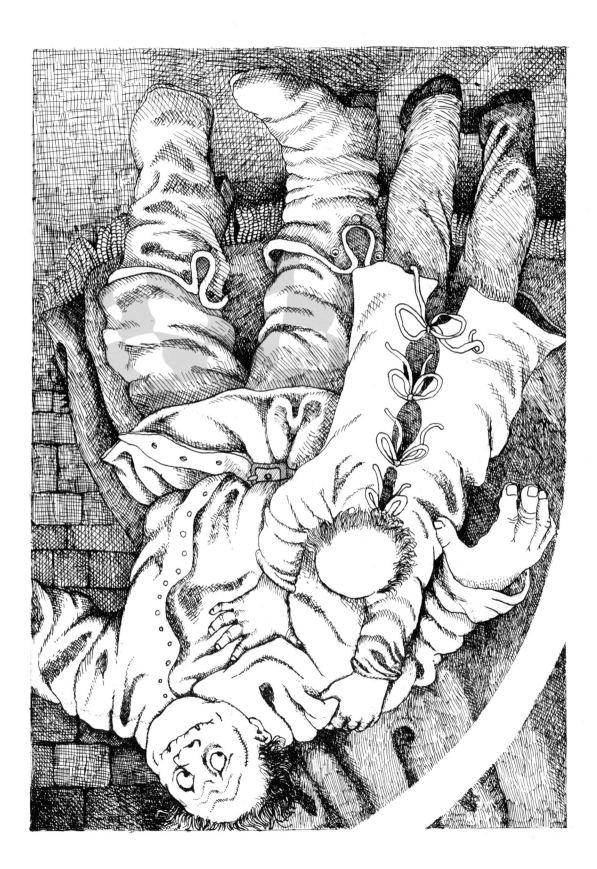

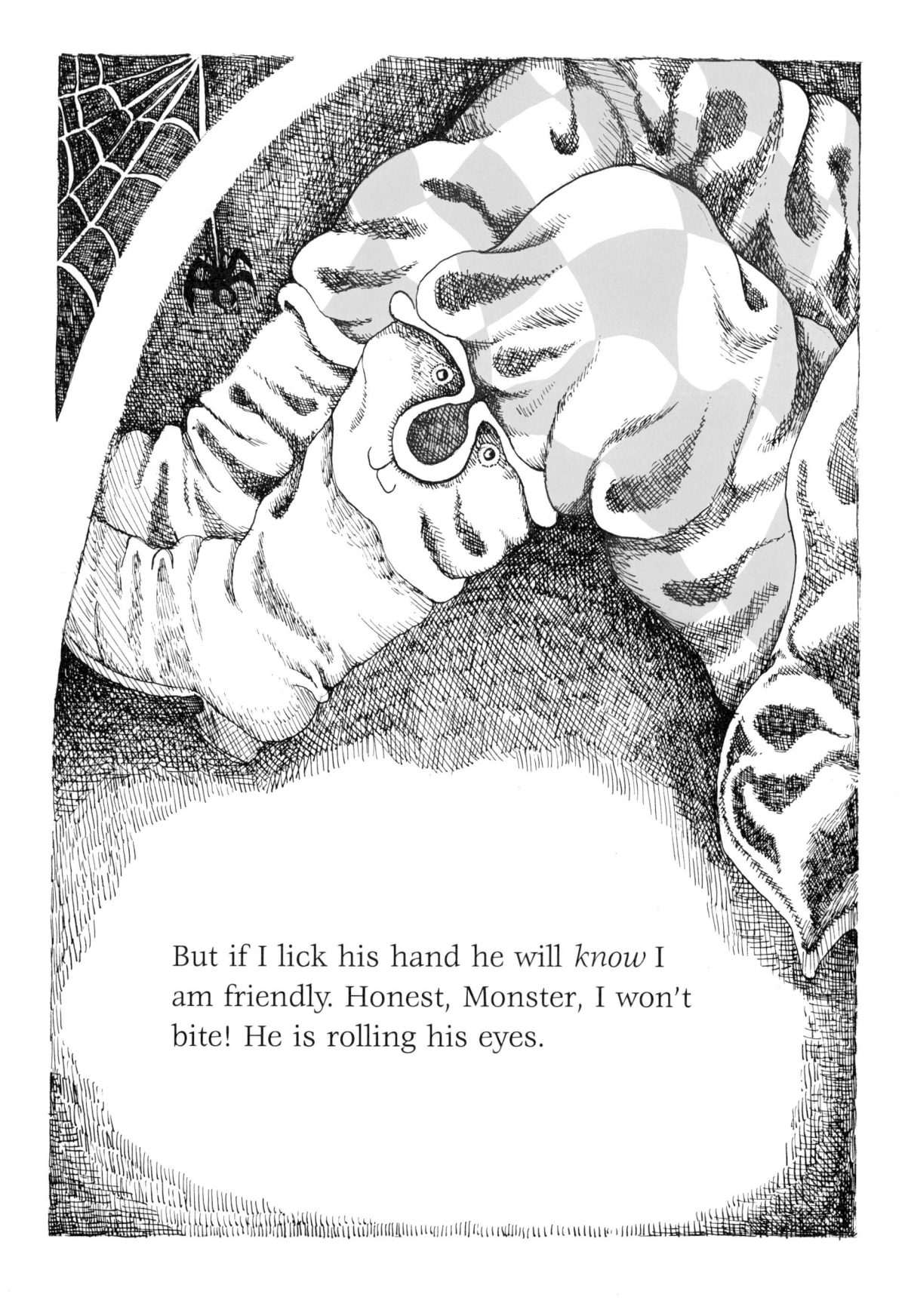

But if I lick his hand he will *know* I
am friendly. Honest, Monster, I won't
bite! He is rolling his eyes.

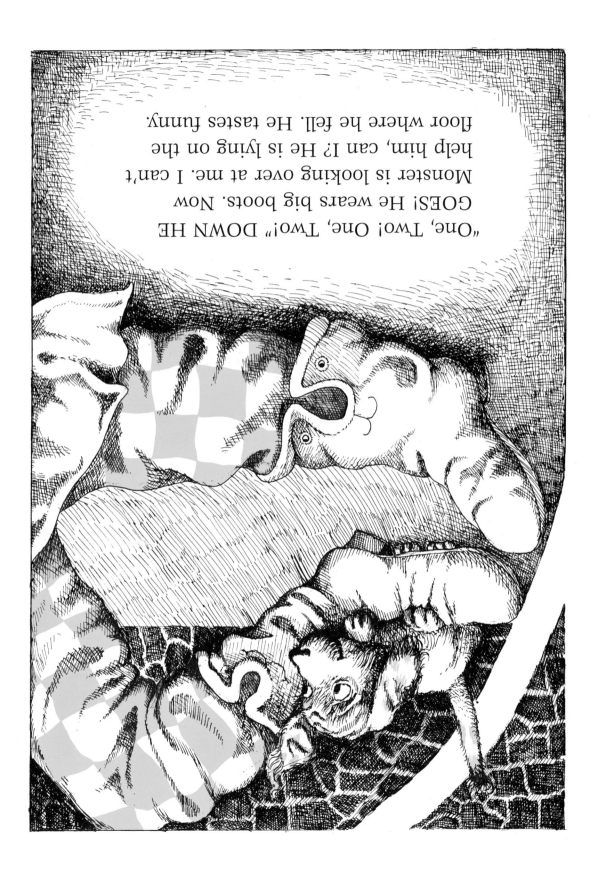

"One, Two! One, Two!" DOWN HE GOES! He wears big boots. Now Monster is looking over at me. I can't help him, can I? He is lying on the floor where he fell. He tastes funny.

Doctor Frankenstein is showing
Monster how to walk. It is hard for
him. Two days old. Watch him walk...
Any puppy can do better than that!
Look at me!

They call it The Monster. *It looks* nice
enough to me. Though I am just a dog.
Frankenstein's dog. "AARRFFF!"

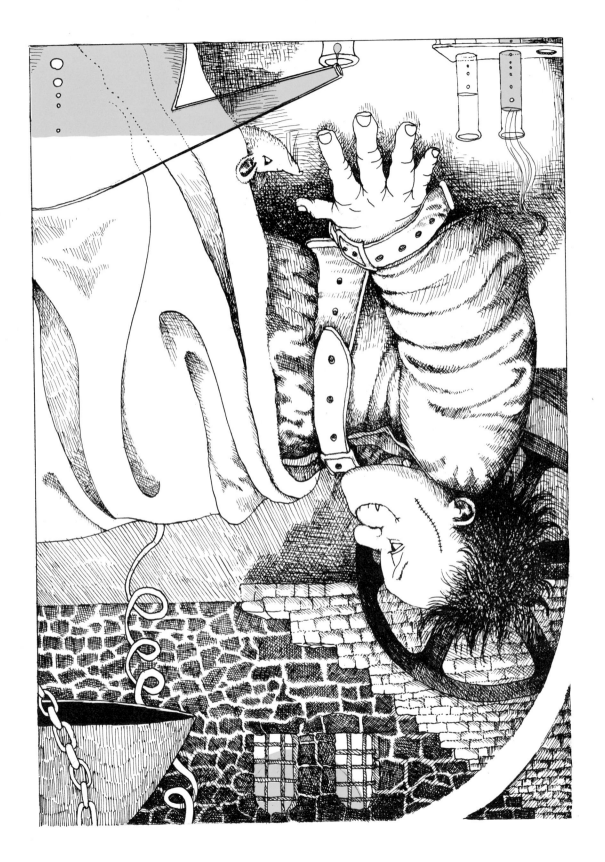

My master, Doctor Frankenstein, is
building a man thing.

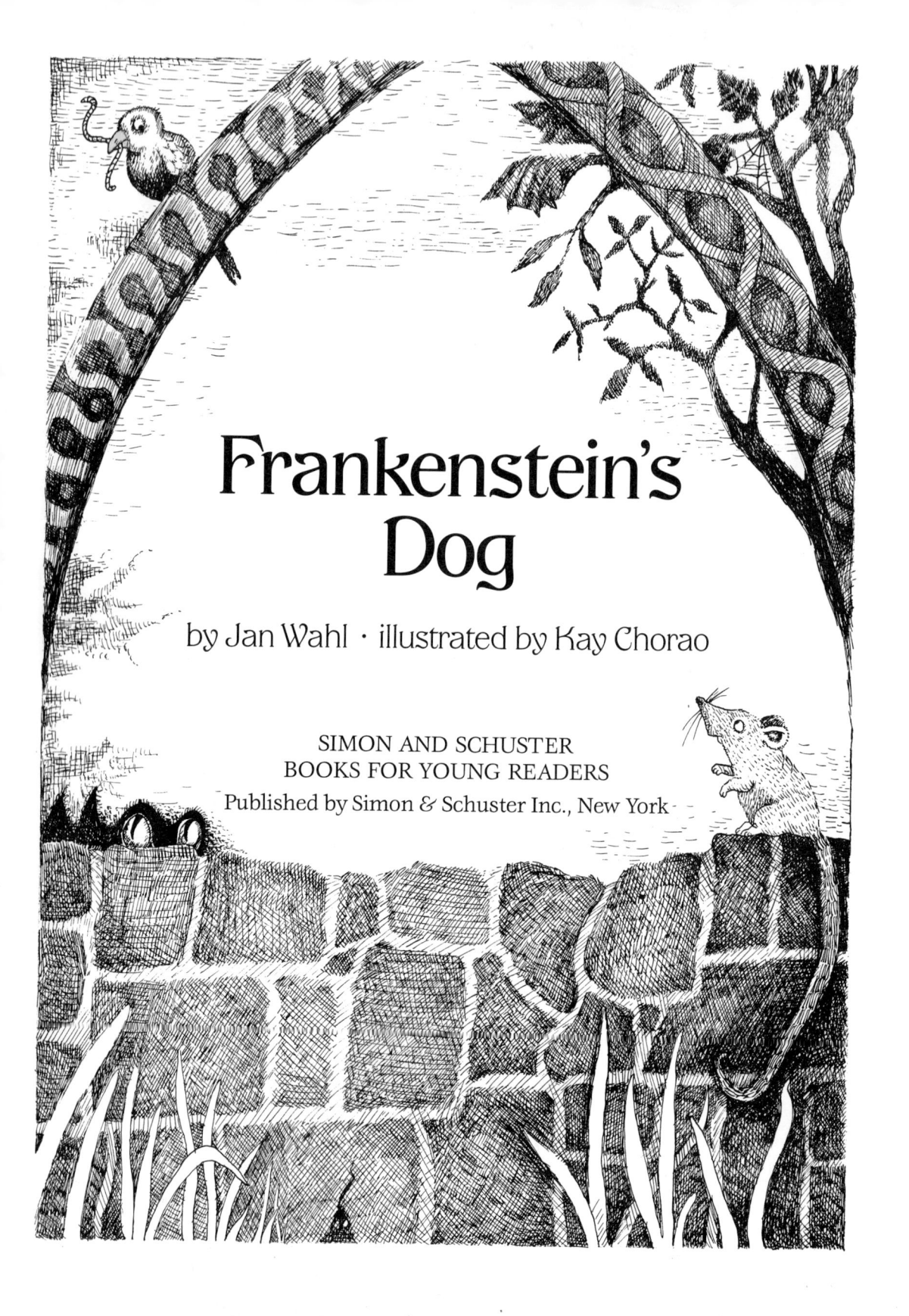

Frankenstein's Dog

by Jan Wahl · illustrated by Kay Chorao

SIMON AND SCHUSTER
BOOKS FOR YOUNG READERS
Published by Simon & Schuster Inc., New York